# Princess G

## and the

# Talking Elephant

## Princess Grumpy and the Talking Elephant

The story was inspired by Karen Engh when she was six years old.

Original Danish version © 2010 Svend-Erik Engh and Lasse Bo Christensen

The English version was written by Svend-Erik Engh and edited by Alice Fernbank

Illustrated by Lasse Bo Christensen

© 2019 Svend-Erik Engh, Alice Fernbank and Lasse Bo Christensen

Forlag: BoD – Books on Demand, København, Danmark
Fremstilling: BoD - Books on Demand GmbH - Norderstedt, Tyskland

**ISBN 9788743009177**

By
Svend-Erik Engh
and
Alice Fernbank

Illustrations
Lasse Bo Christensen

It was Tuesday morning. The King burst into the Princess's bedroom with a big smile on his face, "What a wonderful day it is today! The sun is shining and the world outside is beautiful!"

But the Princess was grumpy, "It's not a wonderful day, and the world is not nice, and one more thing, who put a pea under my mattress? I haven't slept a wink all night, and my body is black and blue."

She was grumpy every morning. In fact she was grumpy every afternoon and every evening too.

The King felt sad as he left her bedroom. It seemed like there was nothing he could do to make her happy.

At the bottom of the bed the Royal Mouse was sitting listening. She loved peas, so when she heard there was a pea in the Princess's bed, she wriggled under the mattress and found it. It was squashed flat, but it still tasted yummy!

The King went to the great meeting hall and sighed as he looked out of the window. He knew exactly why there were no princes lining up to ask for his daughter's hand in marriage. She was so grumpy and nothing could make her laugh.

He tried to think of a solution and he remembered a story he'd once heard about a prince who was riding a goat, while holding a bird and throwing mud around. A princess was watching and she laughed and laughed and thought the prince was charming, so they got married and lived happily ever after.

But the King didn't know any princes with goats, and he didn't want mud spread around his palace, so that was no good.

As the Royal Mouse scuttled by, the King asked her, "What am I going to do about Princess Grumpy?" She looked at the King and shrugged. She didn't know what to do either.

Every Tuesday the ministers met with the King in the great meeting hall to make new laws and solve problems.
The Prime Minister thought that he was the cleverest of all, and every Tuesday he would talk and talk and talk, until everyone fell asleep.
   That Tuesday the Prime Minister was talking as usual, "Blah blah blah…"
And the ministers were sleeping as usual, "zzzzzzzzzz…"
Suddenly the King jumped up and pointed at the Prime Minister, "If you're so clever, tell me what I can do to make my grumpy daughter happy!"
There was a silence, which woke everyone up.
"What happened?" said the Minister of Colours,
"What is going on?" said the Minister of Vegetables,
"Why is it so quiet in here?" said the Minister of Comfy Chairs.
The King explained his problem. Then the Minister of Good Moods spoke up, "Well, why don't you take the Princess to the circus?" she said. "Nothing is more fun!"

So that night the Prime Minister and the King sat beside the Princess watching the clowns tumbling and falling over.

Everyone laughed. Well, almost everyone; the Princess thought the clowns were stupid and that going to the circus was no fun at all.

Then an elephant came into the ring. He was a rather shy elephant, so he just stood there looking at the audience. "Do something funny like the clowns!" someone shouted. "Yes! Make us laugh!" called someone else.
The elephant said softly, "My name is Edgar and I am a talking elephant. Edgar the talking elephant, that's me."

The Princess looked up and a smile spread across her face. She had never imagined that an elephant could talk. She pinched the King's arm and whispered, "A talking elephant. That's amazing!"

But the audience were not happy at all, "Boooo! Hisss!" they called out, and started throwing things at Edgar. Suddenly a shoe hit his head.

"Ouch!" he said.

When the Princess saw this, she marched into the circus ring and shouted, "IF YOU DON'T STOP THROWING THINGS AT EDGAR I WILL CALL FOR AN ARMY OF SOLDIERS!" Everyone went silent.

Then Edgar spoke. "Thank you Princess. It's not fun being a talking elephant when nobody wants to listen."

"No worries." said the Princess as she picked up the shoe and threw it back at the audience.

"OUCH!" came a voice from the darkness.

"I haven't had so much fun in ages," she said. "I love that you're a talking elephant and I'd like to be your friend."

The Princess stroked Edgar's trunk smiling her biggest smile.

The King jumped up and cried, "How much for that elephant?!"

The Circus Ring Master and the King went outside to make a deal.

Edgar and the Princess were already on their way to the palace. He was telling the Princess how much he loved hay. The Princess said, "I once jumped in hay and I had so much fun, but that was a long time ago." She looked sad for a moment, then Edgar said, "I think the smell of hay is the best smell in the world."

"Me too!" said the Princess with a smile, "At the palace I will give you all the hay you want."

The palace stable was full of soft royal hay that smelled like heaven. Edgar and the Princess rolled around in it and laughed until their bellies hurt.

Suddenly the Royal Mouse scuttled by.

"Ahhhhhhh!" shrieked Edgar.

"What's wrong?" said the princess.

"A mouse!" he cried.

"Oh dear," said the Princess, "I'd never have thought that a big elephant like you would be scared of a mouse." But Edgar was trembling, so the Princess tried to distract him.

"Let's sing a song" she said, and she began marching around the stable singing 'Nellie the Elephant'. Edgar smiled and followed her, dancing and trumpeting his trunk.

The King came in and when he saw them dancing and singing he felt so happy. But it was getting late.

"It's bedtime Princess."

"Nooo!" she said "I want to stay and play with Edgar."

"You can come and see Edgar again in the morning."

"I'll be waiting for you." said Edgar and he waved his big ears which made the Princess laugh out loud.

She kissed Edgar goodnight and went up to her bedroom leaving Edgar playing in the hay.

The next morning the King was certain his daughter would be happy and he couldn't wait to wake her up, but when he opened the door the Princess was sitting in bed crying, "Uhhhhhhhhhhhhhuhhhhh!"

"What's wrong?" said the King.

"I've lost my mobile phone!" sobbed the Princess. "I've searched in all my pockets and it's just gone. I don't know what to do!"

"Well we could just get a new one," said the King. "You change phones every time a new model comes out anyway."

"You don't understand. I haven't saved any of the contacts or the pictures or the films or anything else that was on that phone."

The King looked worried.

"I want you and everyone in the palace to look for my phone!" demanded the Princess.

And so the maids, the servants, the butlers, the cooks, the gardeners, the soldiers, and all of the ministers began searching for the Princess's mobile phone.

The search went as far as the stable, where Edgar the elephant was sleeping. They rummaged through the hay around Edgar, which woke him from a dream about royal apples and carrots. He asked in the strangest voice, "Nat id ebrydody nooking for?" He was surprised at the strange sound he made and he cried, "Ohhhh no! Not nabbened to ny noice?" Then he spotted a lump in his trunk and he let out another huge cry, "Oooohhhhh!" He was terrified it was a mouse. This was his worst nightmare.

"Elp!" Edgar cried out, "I av a mouth in my dronk! Elp!" but everyone had gone. Edgar was so scared he fainted.

The Royal Mouse was watching. She jumped down onto Edgar's big body and looked into his trunk to see who was hiding there.

As you know it's the boys with most dirt on their faces who have the best ideas. Well, that's how it is in fairytales. This story is a fairytale and so we have to look for a dirty boy to find a clever person.

In the kitchen there was a boy covered in dirt from top to toe. He had been scrubbing potatoes all of his life. When he heard about the Princess's mobile phone, he said to the king, "Why don't we just call her phone, so we can hear where it is?" The King thought the boy's suggestion was brilliant.

"That boy can think!" he said with a big smile.

Just in that moment the Prime Minister ran by. He was frantically searching for the mobile phone.

"STOP!" shouted the king, and the Prime Minister froze.

"Do you have a plan?" said the King. "Do you have any idea how we can find the Princess's mobile phone?"

"Ermmmm...no," said the Prime Minister.

"Isn't that just the problem? You don't have any new ideas. The Kitchen Boy has just come up with the best idea I've heard for a long time. I think I need a new Prime Minister and this boy is the one for the job. Now please hand over your Prime Minister's uniform."

The Prime Minister took off his suit and handed it to the King.

"Now someone boot this man out of my palace and start running the bath. We have a new Prime Minister and he must be clean!"

"Ouch!" said the old Prime Minister as he landed on the ground outside the door.

He stood up and began walking down the hill, but he wasn't sad at all. Secretly he'd always had a dream of being a baker and he smiled to himself as he thought, "Now I am finally free to bake cakes for the rest of my life."

Meanwhile the new Prime Minister was having a bath and scrubbing a lifetime's worth of potato-dirt from his body.

When he was finished and was clean and dry, he put on the Prime Minister's uniform.

Then he spoke. "Now everyone, silence please while I call the Princess's mobile phone."

The palace was quieter than it had ever been before and the Princess loved it. She thought that the new Prime Minister was the cleverest boy in the world.

Everyone waited and listened, but no-one could hear a phone ringing.

"Oh no!" cried the Princess, "I've just remembered my phone is on silent vibrate mode! I turned it on yesterday when we were at the circus!"

Suddenly there was a loud cry from the stable. Everybody ran down to see what it was.

Edgar was beside himself.

"Elp!" he snuffled, "a nouth ad not nuck in ny nrunk. An now it ith noving around - elp!"

The new Prime Minister looked inside Edgar's trunk and then he smiled a golden smile. "Don't worry, it's not a mouse in there."

"Not ith it den?"

"Well, I think I've just found what we're all looking for."

"My phone!" cried the Princess with a big smile.

The new Prime Minister tickled Edgar under the trunk and he sneezed, "Ahhhchooooo!" The mobile phone shot out. Luckily the new Prime Minister was a good catch. The Princess smiled at the boy as she took the phone. "Thank you!" she said.

"How clever you are!" said the King to the new Prime Minister. "Would you like to marry my daughter?"

"No" said the boy, to the King's surprise.

The Princess looked up from her mobile phone, "We are too young to get married father, you know that."

Then Edgar said, "We don't have time for a wedding now anyway, we are going on an adventure together. Come on everyone!"

The boy took off his Prime Minister's uniform, which didn't fit him anyway, and the three of them packed their bags and went outside.

The Princess climbed onto Edgar's back, the boy handed in his uniform, and they all said farewell to the King as they rode towards the sunset.

The Royal Mouse scuttled after them, and the King smiled and waved as they disappeared over the hills.

THE END